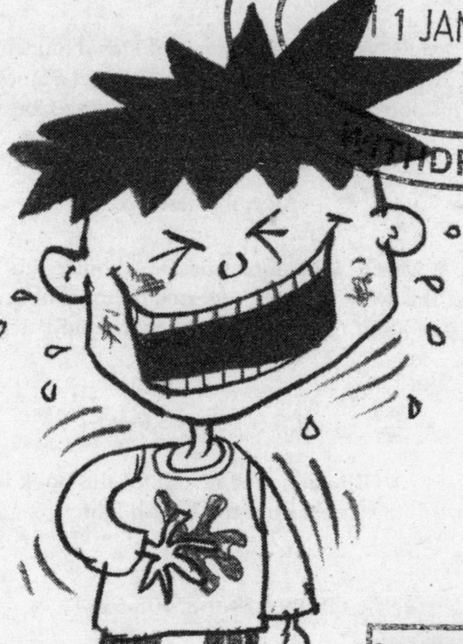

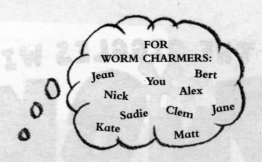

FOR
WORM CHARMERS:
Jean   Bert
   You
Nick   Alex
    Clem   Jane
Sadie
Kate
    Matt

SIMON AND SCHUSTER

First published in Great Britain in 2007
by Simon & Schuster UK Ltd
A CBS COMPANY
1st Floor, 222 Gray's Inn Road, London WC1X 8HB

This edition printed in 2011 exclusively for Books2Door

Text © Matthew Morgan and David Sinden 2007
Cover and inside illustrations © Nigel Baines 2007
This book is copyright under the Berne Convention.
No reproduction without permission.

The right of Matthew Morgan and David Sinden to be identified as
the authors of this work has been asserted by them in accordance with
sections 77 and 78 of the Copyright, Designs and Patents Act, 1988.

1 3 5 7 9 10 8 6 4 2

A CIP catalogue record for this book is
available from the British Library

ISBN 978-0-85707-654-0

Printed and bound by CPI Group (UK) Ltd, Croydon, CR0 4YY

www.simonandschuster.co.uk
www.yuckweb.com

GET THE GIGGLES WITH YUCK

by Matt and Dave

YUCK'S PET WORM

AND

YUCK'S ROTTEN JOKE

Illustrated by Nigel Baines

YUCK'S PET WORM

Yuck was wriggling across the living room carpet. Polly Princess walked in.

"That's disgusting, Yuck," she said.

Yuck was playing with a worm.

He laid his hand on the carpet and the worm wriggled between his fingers and up his arm.

"He's my pet," Yuck said.

"You can't have a worm for a pet.
Worms are disgusting," Polly said.

Yuck gave his worm a stroke. "His
name's Fang."

6

Polly sat on the sofa and opened her copy of *GLITTERGIRL*.

"Why can't you have a normal pet like a bunny or a puppy or a pony? One you can feed or teach tricks or ride."

Fang wriggled over Yuck's tummy.

"I like worms," Yuck said.

Fang wriggled into Yuck's pocket.

"Fang can do anything I tell him to."

"Then tell him to go away," Polly said.

"You're just jealous," Yuck told her, wriggling out of the living room.

"We'll show her, Fang," he whispered.

Yuck wriggled upstairs to the bathroom and grabbed the basket full of dirty laundry. He wriggled to Polly's room and borrowed her recorder from her school bag. Then he wriggled to his bedroom and closed the door. Yuck placed the basket of laundry in the middle of his floor. He took the lid off and dropped Fang on top of the dirty clothes inside.

Fang wriggled through the straps of Mum's bra.

Yuck picked up Polly's recorder and sat cross-legged on the floor. He'd seen it done in a film – a snake charmer had hypnotized a snake.

"Prepare to be hypnotized, Fang," he whispered. He put the recorder to his lips and blew.

The recorder whistled.

"I'm a worm charmer. Come out, come out," Yuck called.

He blew harder.

The recorder squealed.

As Yuck played, Mum's bra began to wriggle.

Yuck kept blowing and, from the top of the basket, a slimy pink head appeared.

"Good boy, Fang," he said.

As Fang heard the sound of the recorder, he wriggled further up out of the laundry.

"You are under my power," Yuck whispered.

Yuck blew higher and higher notes on the recorder.

Fang rose higher out of
the basket, standing tall,
like he was being pulled
by an invisible string.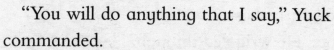

Yuck kept playing.

Fang swayed from side
to side, hypnotized!

"You will do anything that I say," Yuck
commanded.

At that moment, the door flew open. In
walked Polly. "What are you doing with
my recorder?" she asked.

"I was practising."

"But you don't play the recorder," Polly
said. She pointed at Fang. "And what's that
worm doing in the laundry basket?"

Fang was still swaying
from side to side.

"None of your
business," Yuck told her.

Polly snatched the
recorder from Yuck's
hands.

She stomped out of Yuck's room and down the stairs.

Yuck looked at Fang.

Fang was still hypnotized.

"Go and annoy Polly," Yuck commanded.

Fang wriggled down the side of the basket onto the floor. He wriggled through a pair of Yuck's underpants 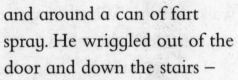 and around a can of fart spray. He wriggled out of the door and down the stairs – tumbling head over tail, down each step and onto the next – until he reached the hallway.

Yuck followed. "Keep going, Fang."

Fang wriggled across the hallway to the living room door.

"Go and annoy Polly," Yuck whispered. Quietly, he nudged open the door and watched as Fang wriggled into the living room.

Polly was sitting on the floor. Her coloured pencils were arranged neatly in front of her.

Fang wriggled across the carpet and lay among them, hiding.

"What are you doing, Polly?" Yuck asked.

"I'm drawing a picture," Polly said.

Polly picked up a pink pencil.

It wriggled in her hand.

"Urrgghh!" she screamed, looking at what she was holding.

The pencil was cold and slimy. It coiled around her finger.

"A worm!"

She jumped up and threw Fang on the floor.

"YUCK!" she screamed, wiping her hand on her dress.

"What?" Yuck said, trying not to laugh.

"Your worm! Your worm was in my pencils!"

"Oh, I was wondering where he'd got to."

Yuck scooped Fang into his hand and stroked him better.

At that moment, Mum came in.

"Mum, Yuck put a worm in my pencils!" Polly cried.

Mum looked at Fang wriggling in Yuck's hand.

"Fang must have escaped," Yuck said. From his pocket he took out a little crumb of mud and gave it to Fang to eat.

"What are you doing with a worm in the house?" Mum asked.

"Fang's my new pet."

"You can't have a worm for a pet. Worms are dirty," Mum said.

"Worms are brilliant!" Yuck told her. He tucked Fang behind his ear, giggled, and ran out of the room.

That night, Yuck took a smelly sock from the top of the laundry basket. He slipped the basket back into the bathroom then laid the sock on his pillow as a sleeping bag for Fang.

The next morning before school, Polly was washing her hair.

While she was in the bathroom, Yuck sneaked to her room. He tiptoed back with her recorder. He sat on his floor and blew. The recorder whistled.

When Fang heard it, he wriggled out of his sleeping bag and stood tall on his tail, swaying from side to side.

Polly stormed into Yuck's room. Her hair was dripping wet.

"That's mine!" she said, snatching the recorder. She slammed the door and went to dry her hair.

Yuck looked at Fang.

Fang was hypnotized.

"Go and annoy Polly," he said.

Fang wriggled across the pillow and down the side of the bed. He wriggled along the floor, over a sick stain and past a slug that had escaped from Slime City.

"That's it, Fang!"

Fang wriggled out of the door, heading for Polly's bedroom.

Polly was sitting at her dressing table brushing her hair.

Fang wriggled across the carpet.

Polly put her hairbrush down and picked up a pink ribbon. She held one side of her hair in a bunch and tied the pink ribbon around it into a bow.

Fang wriggled to her dressing table and climbed up the leg.

Polly held the other side of her hair in a bunch and picked up a second pink ribbon. She tied it into a bow and looked in the mirror. Polly screamed. "UURRGGHH!"

The pink ribbon was wriggling!

Yuck burst into her room.

"What's up?" he asked.

"My hair! My hair! Your worm's in my hair!"

"That looks pretty," Yuck said.

"Get it out! Get it out, Yuck!" Polly screamed.

Trying not to laugh, Yuck carefully untied Fang from Polly's hair and stroked him better.

"Now I'll have to wash my hair again!" Polly shouted, running to the bathroom.

Yuck fed Fang a little crumb of mud.

"Good boy," he said.

He put Fang on the floor. "Go on. Go and annoy Polly."

Fang wriggled downstairs to the hallway and hid among the shoes by the front door.

By the time Polly had washed her hair again and tied her pink ribbons she was late for school.

Dad and Yuck were waiting for her.

"Come on, Polly, hurry up!" Dad called.

"It's Yuck's fault," Polly shouted, running down the stairs. "He put a worm in my hair."

"Fang must have escaped," Yuck said.

As Polly bent down to put her shoes on, Yuck took her recorder from her bag and slipped it into his.

Polly put on one shoe and tied the lace. She put on the other shoe.

The lace felt cold and slimy.

"UURRGGHH!" she screamed.

Fang was wriggling through the holes where her lace should have been.

"YUCK!"

"What is it now, Polly?" Yuck asked.

"It's your worm! Your worm's in my shoe!"

Yuck unpicked Fang from Polly's shoe and fed him another crumb of mud. "I was wondering where he'd got to."

"What are you doing with a worm in the house, Yuck?" Dad asked.

"Fang's my new pet."

"You can't have a worm for a pet. Worms are revolting," Dad said.

"Worms are disgusting!" Polly said.

Yuck gave Fang a stroke. "Fang's great." Then he slipped Fang into his pocket and they left for school.

At breaktime, Yuck and Little Eric were playing in the playground.

Ben Bong was sitting on the bench drinking a carton of Squeeze Juice.

"Watch this," Yuck said, taking Polly's recorder out of his bag.

"But you don't play the recorder," Little Eric said.

Yuck blew into it.

Little Eric watched as a worm wriggled up out of Yuck's pocket. "What's that?"

"His name's Fang. He's my new pet," Yuck said.

Little Eric held his hand out and Fang wriggled onto it.

Fang swayed from side to side.

"What's he doing?" Little Eric asked.

"He's hypnotized," Yuck replied.

Yuck took Fang and placed him on the ground. "Go on. Go and annoy Ben Bong."

Fang wriggled across the playground to where Ben Bong was sitting.

He wriggled up onto the bench.

Ben Bong picked up his carton of Squeeze Juice. He sucked the pink straw. It felt cold and slimy against his lips. Then he felt it wriggle in his mouth.

"UURRGGHH!" Ben Bong screamed.

Yuck and Little Eric laughed.

"A worm!" Ben Bong shouted, dropping his Squeeze Juice. "I just sucked a worm!"

Ben Bong jumped up and ran across the playground to the toilets.

"Can I have a go?" Little Eric asked. He put the recorder to his lips.

"Just blow," Yuck said.

When Fang heard the sound of the recorder he swayed from side to side on the bench.

"Go and annoy the Twinkletrout," Little Eric said.

Yuck and Little Eric watched as Fang wriggled down from the bench and over to the corner of the playground.

Spoilt Jessica and the Twinkletrout were skipping in a circle, playing fairies. Spoilt Jessica was waving a fairy wand, pretending to cast a spell. She tapped the wand on the Twinkletrout's shoulder.

"Is that wand magic?" Little Eric called.

Spoilt Jessica looked at the wand in her
hand. It was pink and slimy.

The Twinkletrout felt it wriggle in her
ear. It felt cold. "UURRGGHH! It's a
worm! There's a worm in my ear!"

Spoilt Jessica dropped Fang on the
ground.

The Twinkletrout ran to the toilets.

Yuck and Little Eric laughed.

"Good boy, Fang," Yuck said, picking
Fang up from the playground. He gave
him a little crumb of mud.

"Worms are brilliant," Little Eric said.

Yuck put Fang in his pocket and slipped
the recorder back into his bag.

That evening, before dinner, Polly was in the kitchen complaining to Mum and Dad.

"It's disgusting," she said. "He spends his whole time with that worm. He even sleeps with it in a sock in his bed!"

"Why has he still got that horrible worm in the house? I told him worms are dirty," Mum said.

"And I told him that worms are revolting," Dad said.

Mum, Dad and Polly looked up as they heard a sound.

"That's my recorder!
He's got it again!" Polly
said. "I've been looking
for it all day."

Yuck strolled in.

Fang's head was poking out of his pocket.

"I was just practising," he said.

"But you've never liked playing the
recorder," Polly told him, snatching the
recorder from him.

Yuck sat down at the table.

"What's for dinner, Mum?" he asked.

"Spaghetti," Mum said.

Yuck dropped Fang down his trouser leg onto the floor under the table.

"Go and annoy Polly," he whispered.

Mum put a big pot of spaghetti on the table and passed the plates round. Polly ladled some spaghetti onto her plate.

Fang wriggled up the table leg. He popped his head over the top of the table, then wriggled across the tablecloth.

Polly scooped up a forkful of spaghetti.

Yuck giggled as he watched her sucking a long pink strand – a long pink SLIMY strand that wriggled and squirmed in her mouth.

"Aarrgghh!" she screamed. Polly spat spaghetti all over the tablecloth.

"Polly!" Mum cried.

"What are you doing?" Dad said to her.

"It's that worm! It's Yuck's worm!"
Everyone looked at the spaghetti spat
out on the tablecloth. Fang was wriggling
among it.

Polly got up from her chair and ran out of the room.

"Where are you going?" Yuck asked.

"To clean my teeth!" Polly shouted.

"Apologise to your sister, Yuck. That was a horrible thing to do," Dad told him.

Yuck picked Fang up off the table and ran out of the kitchen to find Polly.

She was in the bathroom, washing her mouth with soap.

Yuck put Fang down on the edge of the sink. "I've come to say sorry, Polly," he said, trying not to giggle.

Fang wriggled to the pot with the toothbrushes.

"Go away, Yuck. I hate you." Polly was spitting, trying to get the wormy taste out of her mouth. She grabbed the tube of toothpaste and her pink toothbrush from the pot. She squeezed some toothpaste onto her brush. She stuck it in her mouth and started to scrub her teeth.

The toothbrush was all floppy.

It wriggled and squirmed along her gums and tickled her tongue.

She looked in her hand.

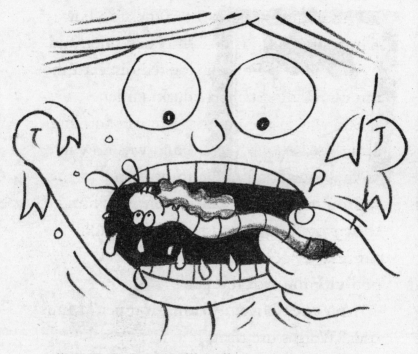

"UURRGGHH!" Polly screamed. She was brushing her teeth with Yuck's worm!

"YUCK!" she yelled. With Fang in her hand, she ran out of the bathroom, down the stairs and through the kitchen, past Mum and Dad.

"NO!" Yuck called, running after her.

"I hate worms!" she shouted, and she threw Fang out of the back door as hard as she could.

Yuck stood at the back door and looked out into the dark garden.

He was too late. Fang was nowhere to be seen.

"You might have killed him," Yuck said.

"It would serve you right!" Polly told him.

"But Fang was my pet."

"You can't have a worm for a pet," Mum said. "Worms are dirty."

"Worms are revolting," Dad said.

"Worms are disgusting," Polly said. She washed her hands and went to her room.

"Now, sit down and finish your dinner, Yuck!" Dad ordered.

"But, Dad…"

"You haven't eaten your spaghetti," Mum said.

Yuck wasn't hungry. He picked at the spaghetti on his plate, but every strand reminded him of Fang.

What if Fang gets eaten by a bird? Yuck thought. What if he wriggles out into the middle of the road?

He had to find Fang.

He had to save him!

After dinner, when Mum and Dad were in the living room watching television, Yuck crept to the cupboard under the stairs and fetched a torch. He sneaked out of the back door into the garden.

"Fang," he called. "Here, boy!"

He shone the torch up and down, over the lawn, over the flower bed. He even searched behind the shed.

But there was no sign of Fang anywhere.

Then, all of a sudden, from high up, Yuck heard the sound of a recorder.

It was Polly. She was practising her recorder in her bedroom. Her window was slightly open and, as she played, the music drifted out over the garden.

Something moved by Yuck's feet.

He shone his torch.

POP! Coming
up out of the
ground was
Fang!

"Here,
boy," Yuck said.
"That's it. Up
you come."

Fang wriggled up out of the ground,
swaying from side to side.

He was hypnotized!

Yuck looked up at Polly's window.

"We'll show her, Fang," he said.

Yuck shone the torch on the drainpipe,
following it up the side of the house to
Polly's open window.

"Go and annoy Polly," Yuck whispered.

As the recorder kept playing, Yuck
noticed something else – there was
something moving in the flower bed.

He shone the torch on it.

POP! Another worm…
It wriggled up out of the
ground, swaying from side to side.
Then another worm popped up…

And another…

Ten worms…

Twenty worms…

A hundred worms…

 A THOUSAND worms!
All hypnotized by the sound of Polly's
recorder.

And Fang was leading them, heading for
the drainpipe.

"Go and annoy Polly," Yuck whispered.
He ran inside.

"I'm going to bed now," he called to Mum and Dad.

Yuck dashed to his room and looked out of his window. The whole garden was a sea of worms, thousands and thousands of them, wriggling and squirming together.

Worms are great! Yuck thought.

Fang was out in front, wriggling up the drainpipe. The rest of the worms were following behind, wriggling up the side of the house, heading for Polly's window.

"Goodnight, Polly," Yuck called. He closed his curtains, tucked himself up in bed and listened.

He could hear Polly packing her recorder back in her bag for the morning, then getting into bed.

He giggled as he heard her switch off her light.

"Sleep well, Polly," he called.

As Yuck lay in his bed he could hear the worms wriggling up the side of the house.

It sounded like the whole wall was moving, the bricks rippling and squelching.

Yuck decided that when he was EMPEROR OF EVERYTHING, worms wouldn't have to live outside in the cold. They would be allowed to live indoors in people's houses, where they could wriggle on the carpet and wriggle on the sofa watching TV. Everyone would have pet worms. He'd have hundreds and he'd give them all names, like The Wriggler or Mr Worm or Squelch.

In the morning, Yuck was woken by a scream from Polly's room.

He ran to her door and looked through the keyhole.

Her room was full of worms.

All through the night they had wriggled in through her window.

Her bed was wriggling with worms.

Worms were on her pillow and in her hair.

Worms squirmed up her nostrils and worms wriggled from her ears.

Worms were everywhere!

"UUURRRGGGHHH!" Polly screamed, clawing with her fingers, pulling the worms from her hair and face.

She sprang out of bed and landed with a sloppy squelch.

Her floor was a deep pit of worms.

They were slithering between her toes and wriggling around her legs, rising higher and higher.

"AAARRRGGGHHH!" she screamed.

Mum and Dad ran to her door.

"What's happening?" they said to Yuck.

"I don't know, I can't see her," Yuck told them, looking through the keyhole.

"Open the door," Dad said.

It wouldn't budge. Something was blocking it.

"What is it, Polly?" Dad called.

"Worms!" she screamed, half scrabbling and half swimming. "My room is full of worms! Help! I'm trapped!"

Yuck could just see her head, poking out of the top of the worms.

"Are you all right, Polly?" Yuck called.

"Noooo!" Polly shouted, "I hate you—!"

But just at that moment, Polly slipped and her head went under.

"What was that, Polly?" Yuck asked. "I can't hear you!"

Polly tried to speak but her mouth was full of worms.

Yuck smiled as one worm slid out through the keyhole.

It wriggled into his hand.

Yuck giggled and gave the worm a stroke. "You're the best pet ever, Fang," he said. "Worms are brilliant!"

YUCK'S ROTTEN JOKE

"What did you bring?" Yuck asked.

It was Monday morning, and Yuck and Little Eric were sitting at the back of assembly rummaging in their bags.

Little Eric pulled out a small brown packet.

"Itching Powder," Yuck read.

Then Little Eric pulled out a small green packet. "And Sneezing Powder."

Yuck took out a Whoopee Cushion, a bottle of Fake Blood and…

"Check this out," he said. From his bag Yuck pulled a curling lump of Dogdidapoo.

Little Eric prodded it with his finger. "It looks just like the real thing."

"Watch this."

Yuck reached forward and put the fake dog poo on the floor in front of him, just where Schoolie Julie was about to sit down.

"Watch out, Schoolie Julie!" Yuck said.

Schoolie Julie sat on the Dogdidapoo and jumped back up.

"Schoolie Julie sat in dog poo!" Little Eric giggled.

"What's going on at the back?" Mr Reaper, the headmaster, boomed.

Yuck quickly put the fake dog poo back in his bag.

"Yuck and Eric, come here!" the Reaper told them.

Yuck and Little Eric walked to the front of assembly.

"Hand me your report cards!" the Reaper said.

From his back pocket, Yuck pulled out a folded piece of orange card.

The Reaper snatched it. "That's a star off for messing about in assembly!"

He held Yuck's report card with his fingertips. Its corners were chewed and the cover was smeared in bogies. As the Reaper opened it, his mouth stretched into a grin. "Well, well, you only have one star for good behaviour."

Sure enough, Yuck's report card only had one star stuck in it.

"When did you get a star?" Little Eric whispered.

"I found it on the floor under the Dragon's desk," Yuck whispered back.

The Reaper peeled the star off, then snatched Little Eric's report card.

Little Eric's had two stars stuck in it.

The Reaper peeled one off.

"I've still got one left!" Little Eric whispered to Yuck.

Then the Reaper peeled off Little Eric's last star. "And that's for whispering!"

He held their empty report cards in the air and showed them to the whole school. "At the end of the week I shall be looking at everyone's report cards. Everyone must have at least ten stars or they will be in BIG TROUBLE – they will be punished and a letter will be sent to their parents."

The Reaper handed the report cards back to Yuck and Little Eric.

After assembly, Polly Princess and Juicy Lucy ran over to Yuck and Little Eric in the playground. Polly was smiling.

"I've got ten stars!" she said, waving her report card in Yuck's face.

"So have I!" said Lucy.

Inside each of their report cards were ten gold stars.

"So what? I've got this," Yuck said. He pulled a plastic flower from his pocket. "Pretty, isn't it?"

Polly looked at the flower.

Yuck squeezed it and smelly pond water squirted in her face.

Little Eric laughed.

That evening, Polly Princess showed Mum and Dad her report card. "Yuck's got no stars and I've got ten. Miss Fortune will probably give me even more tomorrow."

"That's because you're a goodie-goodie," Yuck said. He was sitting at the kitchen table reading *OINK*.

Polly stuck her tongue out at Yuck and stood up to make Mum and Dad a cup of tea.

Yuck turned the page and giggled.

"Why can't you be helpful like your sister?" Mum asked.

"I AM helpful," Yuck said. "I'll help Polly with the tea."

He put down his copy of *OINK*, and from his pocket took out a small plastic packet. On it was written Sugar-Coated Flies. He picked out two lumps and put them in the sugar bowl.

Then he watched as Polly spooned the two sugar lumps into Dad's tea.

"How come you haven't got any stars, Yuck?" Dad asked.

"I have," Yuck said.

Polly handed Mum and Dad their tea. "He's lying."

"Show me your report card, Yuck," Dad told him, taking a sip from his mug.

Yuck rummaged in his pocket. "I must have left it at school."

At that moment, Dad coughed and spat out his tea, spraying it across the room.

"Flies! Polly, there are flies in my tea!" he shouted.

"It wasn't me! It must have been Yuck!"
Polly said.

But Yuck was already running up the stairs. He threw himself on his bed and emptied his jokes from his bag.

Yuck decided that when he was EMPEROR OF EVERYTHING people would be given stars for playing jokes. He and Little Eric would have hundreds. Goodie-goodies would have none. And the Reaper would be in BIG TROUBLE because he never played jokes and he was never ever funny. He'd get no stars at all, and for his punishment he'd be turned into a giant dog poo.

At Tuesday breaktime, Yuck and Little Eric sat in a tree at the edge of the playground. They were looking down at a coin that they had glued to the ground.

"Do you really think we can get five stars?" Little Eric asked.

"It's Polly and Lucy who are going to be in BIG TROUBLE," Yuck said.

He had a plan.

Polly Princess and Juicy Lucy were walking to their classroom.

"Ssshhh! They're coming," Little Eric whispered.

Polly spied the coin on the ground and ran over. But when she bent down to pick it up, the coin wouldn't budge.

In the tree, Yuck opened the packet of Sneezing Powder. Little Eric opened the packet of Itching Powder. While Polly struggled with the coin, they sprinkled the powder over her.

"It's stuck," Polly said to Lucy.

"ATCHOO!" She was scratching her hair.

"Let me try," Lucy said, bending down to pick up the coin. She dug her nails under it, trying to prise it from the ground.

Yuck and Little Eric sprinkled the powder on her.

"It won't move. ATCHOO!" She was scratching her neck. "We'd better get going or—ATCHOO!—we'll be late for class!"

Polly and Lucy sneezed and scratched across the playground, pushing past everyone as the bell rang for lessons. They were still sneezing and scratching when they ran into class.

"ATCHOO!"

Miss Fortune looked over her glasses at them. "Is something wrong?"

"Nothing, Miss," Polly said, scratching her head. "ATCHOO!"

"We're fine, Miss," Lucy said, scratching her tummy. "ATCHOO!"

"Stop fidgeting," Miss Fortune told them.

But no matter how hard they tried, Polly and Lucy couldn't sit still.

"Is this some kind of joke?" Miss Fortune asked.

"I feel—all—itchy—ATCHOO!" Polly said.

Polly and Lucy stood up and began scratching one another.

"You're behaving like a couple of chimpanzees!" Miss Fortune said. "Stop it this minute!"

But Polly and Lucy couldn't stop sneezing and they couldn't stop scratching.

"Hand me your report cards!" Miss Fortune shouted.

Polly and Lucy took out their report cards and handed them to Miss Fortune.

"I'm surprised at you two."

"ATCHOO!" Polly and Lucy both sneezed over Miss Fortune.

Miss Fortune wiped her face and took a star from each of them.

"But Miss!" Polly moaned. "It's not our fault—ATCHOO!"

At that moment, there was a knock at the classroom door.

It was Yuck and Little Eric.

"Sorry to interrupt, Miss," Yuck said.

"Why aren't you in your lesson?" Miss Fortune asked.

"Because we've come to report a lost coin, Miss."

"We've been guarding it," Little Eric said, "in case of thieves."

"Where is it?"

"In the playground. Polly and Lucy dropped it when they were swinging in the trees."

"We didn't want to pick it up because it isn't ours, Miss," Yuck said.

"That was very good of you," Miss Fortune said. "Polly and Lucy can collect it at lunchbreak. Here, you can have these."

Miss Fortune licked the two stars that she'd taken from Polly and Lucy, and stuck them into Yuck and Little Eric's report cards.

They ran off giggling. "We've got one! We've got one star each! Only nine more to go!"

At lunchtime, Polly and Lucy had to take off their itchy clothes and change into their gym kit. When they went outside to fetch the coin, it had gone. So instead, they decided to play catch.

"I bet it was Yuck," Polly said, throwing the ball.

"I want my star back," Lucy said, catching the ball. "I've only got nine left."

"Yuck's going to be in BIG TROUBLE for this!"

Yuck and Little Eric were alone in Mrs Wagon the Dragon's classroom — she had gone to lunch. They were standing at the window watching Polly and Lucy.

Yuck took a clear strip of sticky tape from his bag. He drew a jagged black line across it, like a crack, and stuck it to the window.

As the Reaper came round the corner on playground patrol, Yuck and Little Eric ran outside.

"Sir, Sir, there's been an accident!" Little Eric called. "I don't know what happened exactly, but we were just doing some extra work in the Dragon's, I mean Mrs Wagon's, room when we heard the sound of breaking glass!"

"What's that, Sir?" Yuck said, looking at the window with the crack stuck across it.

The Reaper pointed. "A broken window!" he boomed. "Mrs Wagon will be furious!"

The Reaper looked over at Polly and Lucy playing catch. "Did you do this?" he asked.

"It wasn't us, Sir!"

"Don't tell fibs. You must have smashed it with your ball. Give me your report cards."

The Reaper took a star each from Polly and Lucy's cards.

"But Sir!" Polly said.

The Reaper turned to Yuck and Little Eric. "You two can have these for being good and doing extra work at lunchtime."

He stuck Polly and Lucy's stars into Yuck and Little Eric's report cards.

"That's not fair!" Lucy said.

Yuck and Little Eric ran off giggling. "We've got two! We've got two stars each! Only eight more to go!"

On Wednesday, Polly and Lucy were tidying the books on Miss Fortune's bookshelf. From the corridor they heard shouting.

"Help!"

"Aarrgghh!"

The girls held each other tightly as the classroom door burst open. It was Yuck and Little Eric. "Help!" they cried. "Help!"

The girls screamed.

Blood was running down Yuck's face. His cheek had a long red scar across it.

Little Eric's ear was hanging off the side of his head.

"Help us!" Yuck cried.

"We've been attacked by a squirrel!" Little Eric added.

"A really big one!" Yuck said, staggering over to Polly and Lucy. "Help! I'm going to faint."

Polly grabbed Yuck's arm to steady him.
The arm came off in her hand.
She screamed.

Little Eric pointed to the door with a
blood-squirting severed finger. "Nurse
Payne! Get Nurse Payne!"

Little Eric closed his eyes and clutched his head.

An eyeball rolled across the floor.

Polly and Lucy screamed and ran out of the room, down the corridor, all the way to Nurse Payne. "It's Yuck and Little Eric. They've been attacked by a squirrel!"

"By a WHAT?"

"A really big one! Quick! Come quick!"

Nurse Payne grabbed her First-Aid box.

Back in Miss Fortune's classroom, Yuck picked up his Fake Severed Arm and Little Eric picked up his Fake Eyeball. They laughed and wiped the Fake Blood from their faces.

Little Eric put the Fake Severed Ear and the Fake Severed Finger back in his pocket.

They heard footsteps, and pretended to tidy the books on the bookshelf.

"Your scar!" Little Eric said.

Yuck peeled the Fake Scar from his face just as Polly, Lucy and Nurse Payne ran into the room.

"What's going on?" Polly asked. "Where's
the blood gone?"

"What are you talking about?" Yuck
said. "Little Eric and I were just tidying the
shelves for Miss Fortune."

Nurse Payne turned to Polly and Lucy.
"I think you two have some explaining
to do."

Miss Fortune came in. "What's
happening here?" she asked.

"These two girls have been playing
tricks," Nurse Payne told her. "They said
Yuck and Eric were attacked
by a giant squirrel."

"But they were, Miss."

"Ridiculous! Hand me your report cards!" Miss Fortune said. She took a star each from Polly and Lucy's report cards.

"And what are these two doing in here?" she said, looking at Yuck and Little Eric.

"They were just tidying your books for you," Nurse Payne told her.

"What a nice surprise," Miss Fortune said, and she stuck Polly and Lucy's stars into Yuck and Little Eric's report cards. "That was very thoughtful of you."

Yuck and Little Eric laughed and ran off down the corridor.

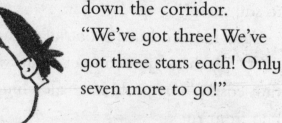

"We've got three! We've got three stars each! Only seven more to go!"

At lunchtime, in the canteen, Polly and Lucy were moaning.

"It's not fair!" Polly said. "They're getting all our stars! I've only got seven left."

Yuck and Little Eric walked over.

"We just wanted to say sorry for what happened earlier," Yuck said.

"It was only meant to be a joke," Little Eric said.

"Then give our stars back," Lucy told them.

"How about we give you these instead, to say sorry?"

Yuck handed Lucy a bag of sweets.

"Don't think you can get away with it that easily," Lucy told him, snatching the bag from Yuck.

"We know what you're up to," Polly said, unwrapping a sweet and chewing it. "And when the Reaper finds out he'll take away ALL your stars and you'll be in BIG TROUBLE."

Yuck and Little Eric went and sat down.

"I didn't know you had sweets," Little Eric said.

"Not ordinary sweets – Extra-hot Sweets!" Yuck said.

By the time Polly and Lucy had got their lunch and sat down at their table, they'd both eaten three sweets each.

"Do you feel a bit hot?" Polly asked. "My mouth's burning."

"I feel... ON FIRE!" Lucy replied. Sweat was pouring down her face.

From his bag Little Eric took out what looked like a lumpy plastic puddle. "Fake Sick. Watch this."

Little Eric sneaked the Fake Sick onto the table next to Polly.

Her face was bright purple. "I feel ill," she said.

"Me too," Lucy said, and she pointed. "Is that what I think it is?"

"It looks like—BLURGH!"

Polly was sick in her hands.

Lucy was sick on Polly.

Mrs Dollop the dinner-lady ran over.

"What have you been eating?" she asked.

Polly couldn't speak. She threw the bag of sweets on the table.

Little Eric glanced at Yuck and gave him a thumbs-up.

Yuck ran out to the playground to find the Reaper. "Polly and Lucy have been sick, Sir," he said.

Meanwhile, Little Eric picked up the Fake Sick, wiped it clean and put it back in his bag.

The Reaper came running in. He looked at the sick all over the table and then at the bag of sweets. "Polly and Lucy! That's a star off for each of you, for eating sweets before lunch!"

"But Sir…" Polly gasped.

The Reaper took a star from Polly and Lucy's report cards. "Now, go and clean yourselves up, you greedy girls."

Yuck picked up the bag of Extra-hot Sweets from the table, holding his hand over the label. "Do you want Polly's sweets, Sir?"

"I expect you'll want to confiscate them," Little Eric said.

"Good idea," the Reaper said.

He took the bag of sweets and gave Yuck and Little Eric a star each for being helpful. Then he went back outside to patrol the playground.

Yuck and Little Eric watched from the window, giggling as the Reaper unwrapped a sweet and popped it into his mouth.

"We've got four! We've got four stars each! Only six more to go!"

On Thursday, Yuck and Little Eric arrived early at school.

They were first to assembly. As Polly sat down, Yuck slipped a Whoopee Cushion underneath her bottom.

RRRRRRRRIP! It let off a loud raspberry.

Polly jumped up and Yuck cracked a Stink Bomb.

"What's going on over there?" the Reaper boomed.

"Polly farted, Sir," Yuck said.

"It smells, Sir!" Little Eric said.

Lucy pulled the Whoopee Cushion from underneath Polly and held it up.

"It was this, Sir," she said.

"You know it's forbidden to play practical jokes in school!"

"But it's not mine, Sir!" Lucy said.

Yuck slipped the packet of Stink Bombs into Polly's bag.

The Reaper ran over, holding his nose.

"Haven't you two caused enough trouble this week?" he said to Polly and Lucy.

"But it wasn't us!"

"Empty your bags!"

Polly and Lucy turned their bags upside down.

"See, Sir, just books and a hairbrush and our pencil cases and—"

"Stink Bombs!" the Reaper boomed. "Right, that's another star off for each of you."

"But it's him, Sir — it's all Yuck's fault," Polly protested.

Yuck and Little Eric stood up. "Can we have a star please, Sir?"

"What for?"

"For opening all the windows, Sir," Yuck said. "It stinks in here!"

"That's very thoughtful of you. Here, you can have one star each."

Assembly was evacuated while the stink cleared.

"We've got five! We've got five stars each!" Yuck and Little Eric ran around the playground.

"I've never had five stars before!" Little Eric said.

"Soon we'll have ten stars each," Yuck said.

"How?" Little Eric asked.

"We'll play a big joke – a big ROTTEN JOKE!" Yuck said.

He whispered something into Little Eric's ear, and Little Eric giggled.

For the rest of the day Polly and Lucy stayed in Miss Fortune's classroom.

"It's not fair. Yuck and Little Eric have got as many stars as us now!" Lucy said.

Polly whispered in Lucy's ear: "I know how we can get them back…"

On Friday, Polly and Lucy went spying.

"We'll catch them red-handed," Polly said. "When the Reaper finds out what they've been up to, Yuck and Little Eric will be in BIG TROUBLE."

In assembly, they saw Yuck and Little Eric giggling.

"They're planning another joke," Polly said.

During breaktime, Polly and Lucy saw
Yuck and Little Eric go to Mr Sweep's store
cupboard and fetch a bucket.

"What do you think they're doing with
Sweepy's bucket?" Lucy asked.

At lunchtime Polly and Lucy followed
Yuck and Little Eric round the back of the
kitchens and watched as they filled the
bucket with
the week's
leftovers:
custard and
baked beans,
yoghurt and
chips, lumpy
gravy, cheesy
pizza – and
ROTTEN EGGS!

"Now we need to hide it," Polly and
Lucy heard Yuck say. "Until after lunch."

"Where?" Little Eric asked.

"The Reaper's office!" Yuck said.

"Are you crazy?"

"The Reaper's on playground patrol all
lunchtime. It's the last place anyone will
look. We'll fetch it when the bell goes and
gunk Polly and Lucy on their way into
class."

Polly and Lucy looked at one another.
"We've got them!" Lucy said.

They followed Yuck and Little Eric to the
Reaper's office, then hid behind a large
plant in the corridor and watched as Yuck
nudged the door open.

"It's all clear," he said.

Yuck and Little Eric crept inside and closed the door behind them.

"Did they follow us?" Little Eric whispered.

"They've been following us all morning," Yuck whispered back.

Polly and Lucy tiptoed out from behind the plant, pressed their ears to the door and listened.

Inside, in a loud voice, Yuck was speaking: "Let's hide the bucket under the desk. When the bell goes we'll collect it, and then gunk Polly and Lucy on their way into class."

"But how are we going to gunk them without being seen?" Little Eric asked loudly.

"We'll balance the bucket on top of their classroom door. Polly and Lucy are always first to class. They'll get covered."

Polly and Lucy looked at one another.

The door handle turned.

"Quick, hide!" Polly whispered.

Polly and Lucy hid behind the plant as Yuck and Little Eric came out of the Reaper's office and wandered off down the corridor.

Polly and Lucy sneaked inside.

They looked under the Reaper's desk.

"There's the bucket," Lucy said. "Let's tell on them."

"We'll do better than that," Polly said.

She pointed at the door. "You heard what they said. They'll be coming back later. Quick – get the bucket!"

Polly stood on a chair next to the door and Lucy handed the bucket up to her.

"When they come back to fetch it, they'll get gunked!" Polly said.

She opened the door just a little bit and stretched as high as she could, balancing the bucket on top of the door.

"Perfect!" Lucy said.

"And when the Reaper sees them, he'll tell them off for messing about in his office. They'll be in BIG TROUBLE!"

"And we'll get stars for catching them," Lucy said.

Polly and Lucy hid under the Reaper's desk and waited.

"Sshhh!" Polly said. "I can hear them coming."

Yuck and Little Eric were walking back along the corridor.

"What are they doing with a bucket in my office?" the Reaper was asking.

"I don't know. But they looked like they were up to no good," Yuck said.

The door to the Reaper's office was slightly open.

The Reaper took a step forward and pushed on the handle.

Yuck and Little Eric took a step back.

As the door swung open, the bucket fell on the Reaper's head with a SPLASH!

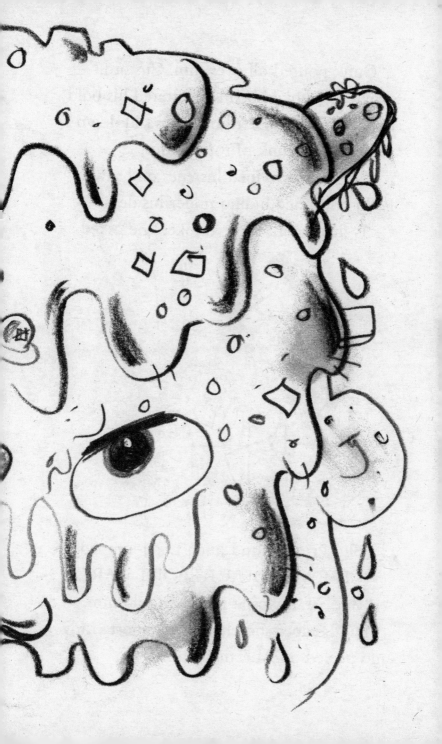

Gunk poured all over him. Custard, gravy and baked beans splattered his bald head. Pizza, yoghurt and chips slid down his face. He stank of rotten eggs!

The Reaper wiped his eyes and saw Polly and Lucy hiding under his desk.

"Is this meant to be a joke?" he asked.

Polly Princess and Juicy Lucy jumped up. "GIVE ME YOUR REPORT CARDS!"

"But, Sir, it wasn't us!" they told him.

The Reaper snatched their report cards and peeled off ALL their stars.

"Polly and Lucy, you are in BIG TROUBLE!" he said. "I shall be writing to your parents immediately!"

"Do we get a reward, Sir?" Yuck asked. "For helping you catch them."

The Reaper stuck Lucy's stars in Little Eric's report card and Polly's stars in Yuck's.

"We've got ten!" Yuck said. "We've got ten stars each!"

GET THE GIGGLES WITH ALL YUCK'S BOOKS!

YUCK'S SLIME MONSTER
(and Yuck's Gross Party)
YUCK'S AMAZING UNDERPANTS
(and Yuck's Scary Spider)
YUCK'S PET WORM
(and Yuck's Rotten Joke)
YUCK'S MEGA MAGIC WAND
(and Yuck's Pirate Treasure)
YUCK'S FART CLUB
(and Yuck's Sick Trick)
YUCK'S ALIEN ADVENTURE
(and Yuck's Slobbery Dog)
YUCK'S ABOMINABLE BURP BLASTER
(and Yuck's Remote Control Revenge)
YUCK'S BIG BOGEYS
(and Yuck's Smelly Socks)
YUCK'S SUPERCOOL SNOTMAN
(and Yuck's Dream Machine)
YUCK'S ROBOTIC BOTTOM
(and Yuck's Wild Weekend)
YUCK'S CRAZY CHRISTMAS
(and Yuck's Naughty New Year)
YUCK'S FANTASTIC FOOTBALL MATCH
(and Yuck's Creepy Crawlies)

Join Yuck's fanclub at
YUCKWEB.COM